Only Molly

If you enjoy reading this book, you
might also like to try another story
from the MAMMOTH STORYBOOK series:

Magic Betsey Malorie Blackman

Betsey's Birthday Surprise Malorie Blackman

A School forAmos Elana Bregin

Blair the Winner! Theresa Breslin

Oh, Omar! Lisa Bruce

Allie's Apples Helen Dunmore

Tricky Tricky Twins Kate Elizabeth Ernest

A Dog for Life Felicity Everett

Kamla and Kate Jamila Gavin

Pest Friends Pippa Goodhart

Hot Dog, Cool Cat Jenny Nimmo

Connie and the Water Babies Jacqueline Wilson

Only Molly

Cally Poplak

illustrated by Alison Bartlett

mammoth

For my mother

C.P.

To Paul and Shona,
many thanks and much love

A.B.

First published in Great Britain in 1998
by Mammoth, an imprint of Egmont Children's Books Limited
Michelin House, 81 Fulham Road, London SW3 6RB

Text copyright © 1998 Cally Poplak
Illustrations copyright © 1998 Alison Bartlett

The rights of Cally Poplak and Alison Bartlett to be identified as
the author and illustrator of this work have been asserted by them
in accordance with the Copyright, Designs and Patents Act 1988

ISBN 0 7497 3183 4

10 9 8 7 6 5 4

A CIP catalogue record for this book
is available from the British Library

Printed in Great Britain by Cox & Wyman Ltd,
Reading, Berkshire

Contents

~

1 *An unwanted visitor*

'So, Molly, what mouth-watering, nose-twitching, finger-licken' treat have you brought home to poison . . .'

'Mum!'

'I mean, feed me with, today?'

Molly and her mum were walking home from school.

'Actually, my biscuits last week were only a little bit burnt. Benjy loved them.'

Molly's mum gasped. 'Now you tell

me – I didn't realise they were dog biscuits.'

'You silly-billy,' Molly giggled. 'You're not getting one of my rock cakes now ...'

'Poor you! Your arm must be so tired, carrying all those rocks in your schoolbag.'

'Mu-um,' Molly groaned. 'They're not real rocks.'

'If they're as heavy as your flapjacks, they are,' her mum laughed, squeezing Molly's hand affectionately.

'Actually, they're as light as a feather – see?' Molly swung her schoolbag back

and forth, puffing her cheeks out because the cakes *were* rather heavy. Unfortunately, she didn't notice the cracked paving stone . . .

'Oops!' her mum just caught her before she fell over.

'Well, perhaps not that light,' Molly admitted. 'But they've got sticky currants in them. Those *are* a little burnt – the ones on the outside, anyway – but I can pick most of them off for you.'

Molly's mum laughed. 'I'm sure they're scrumptious.'

Molly let go of her mum's hand and ran ahead. They were already at the corner of their street. Molly and her mum lived on the ground floor of a house, which had been turned into two flats. Rosie and Tim lived upstairs.

Molly's mum caught up with her at the front door and let her in. Molly skipped to the door of their flat.

'Naughty you, Mum. You didn't lock the door properly . . . Hello, Tim, what are you doing . . . ?' Molly just had time to see Tim and a policeman standing in the sitting-room, before her mum yanked her away.

'Oww!' Molly pulled a face and rubbed her arm.

'Wait outside, Molly. See if Mrs Willis is in next door.'

'I don't want to see Mrs . . .'

'Molly! Do as you're told!'

'Actually, you don't have to SHOUT,' Molly shouted, blinking back tears.

'I'm sorry. Please just wait outside a minute.' She kissed Molly's head and gently pushed her out of the front door.

Molly leant against the wall. 'I'm not going to see Mrs Willis.' She started to pick at her shirt sleeve. 'I want to talk to the policeman.' She kicked a stone at a tree, then tiptoed back to the flat. She could see Tim talking to the policeman, and her mum . . . Was Mum crying?

Molly pushed open the door. 'Mum. What's . . . who's . . .' Molly's mouth opened and closed, but no sound came out. Her tummy was churning just like it did on long, swervy car journeys.

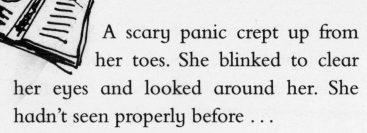

A scary panic crept up from her toes. She blinked to clear her eyes and looked around her. She hadn't seen properly before ...

The room was upside down. All the books had been pulled off the shelves. The sofa cushions were in tatters, spewing out feathers. The drawers from the writing-desk were on the floor, their contents scattered about. The pictures were crooked on the walls. The television was ... where?

Molly's comfy sitting-room was gone.

She saw the policeman standing by the window, a notepad in his hand. Her mum was sitting on the edge of the armchair, cuddling a cushion. She looked very quiet and very pale. Molly had never seen her like that before.

Tim picked Molly up in a big bear hug. 'It's all right, Molly. The burglar's gone. We'll soon have the room back to normal.' He stroked her hair. 'Why don't you come upstairs for a while? Rosie will be back from work in a minute.'

Molly was crying now. Big, fat tears rolled down her cheeks and her nose started to run. Where was James? Were her toys safe? What about her room . . .?

Molly loved her room. She had chosen the colours herself. It was painted a warm, cosy yellow, with yellow-and-white striped curtains. There was a big, puffy duvet to match and a velvety bright green beanbag in the corner.

Molly wriggled out of Tim's arms. She rubbed her eyes with the back of her

hands, then gave a big sniff and wiped her nose on her sleeve. Feeling a little fuzzy, she went through to her bedroom. She hardly dared look . . .

Very slowly, and holding her breath, Molly went in. She rubbed her eyes again and let out her breath.

Her teddies were huddled together on the beanbag. Her piggy bank was on her bedside table. Her books were crammed on to three shelves. Everything was just as she'd left it. She could even see the pyjamas stuffed behind the curtains, where she'd kicked them this morning. Only one thing was missing: no James on her bed.

James was Molly's cat. He was black and white and rather large. He liked to be stroked and cuddled, but he didn't like strangers and he hated other cats. He would often come home after being out all night with a torn ear or a scratched nose. Molly would try to tell him off for picking fights with other cats, but he would rub against her leg, purring and mewing, begging to be picked up, and Molly would always forgive him.

'James,' she called, tears welling up again.

A pitiful mewing came from under the bed. Molly crouched down and saw her startled cat squashed against the wall, tail twitching.

'It's all right, James. The burglar's gone. We'll soon have everything back to normal.' James crept out from his hiding-place. Molly picked him up and rubbed

her face next to his familiar-smelling body. 'You kept my room safe, didn't you?' James nudged her ear and Molly giggled with relief.

Molly's mum came in. 'You found him.' She crouched down and gave Molly a hug.

'Are you OK, Mum?'

'I am now,' she smiled through wet

eyes. She brushed Molly's hair out of her sticky face and kissed her cheek. She found a clean tissue in her pocket and tore it in half. 'Half for you and half for me,' she said, then blew her nose.

Molly put James on her bed. 'You're all right now, aren't you, James?' Then she took her mum's hand and led her back to the sitting-room. 'I'll help you tidy up,' she said. Her mum hated tidying up.

The policeman had gone. Tim was putting the books back on the shelves.

Molly spotted her mum's favourite vase on the floor. The dried lavender had spilled out of it, but the vase was still in one piece. Somehow, that made everything seem all right.

Molly picked up the vase. 'Look, Mum.'

She could see her mum was about to cry again. 'What you need is a nice cup of strong, black tea,' Molly said. 'Maybe with sugar.' Mrs Willis always said a good cup of strong, black tea made you feel better. But Molly couldn't remember if you had to have sugar in it.

'That's sounds like an excellent idea,' said Tim. 'Let's all go upstairs. We can clear up later.'

Her mum smiled gratefully. 'You know what, Molly? A cup of tea is just what I fancy. But there's only one thing that will really make me feel better ...'

Molly frowned.

'... One of your rock cakes.' She tickled Molly's stomach. 'Especially the burnt bits!'

2 Boring old Aunt Jan

Mrs Willis opened her front door and saw a large cardboard box.

'Mrs Willis, please may I have this box?' asked Molly who was holding the box, which was almost as big as her.

'Of course, Molly. Why are you asking me?'

'Because it was next to your dustbin. Isn't it yours?'

'Well, no . . .'

'Maybe it belongs to Tim and Rosie.'

'I wouldn't worry, Molly. If someone left it by the bin, I'm sure they don't want it any more.'

Molly chewed her lip. 'But, Mrs Willis, taking something that isn't yours is bad. It's burglary.'

Mrs Willis gave Molly a sort-of-hug – the box didn't make it very easy. Usually Molly liked to be hugged. Big bear hugs, like Tim gave her or soft, cotton-wool hugs like Mum gave her. But just now she wished Mrs Willis would be careful of the box.

'Actually, Mrs Willis, I think you're squashing the box . . .'

Mrs Willis laughed. 'Come on, you. Come inside and tell me what you want with that cardboard box.'

Molly was supposed to be getting ready to go out. She didn't want to go out. Also, she didn't want to hurt Mrs Willis's feelings. 'OK, but I can only spare a moment.'

Benjy, Mrs Willis's dog, dashed out of his basket to greet Molly. He bounced up and down excitedly.

'Ooh, Benjy! You're going to spoil my box, silly-billy.' Molly put the box down and let the terrier leap into her arms. She screwed up her face as he licked her cheeks. 'Yuck! No wonder Mum always makes me have a bath,' Molly giggled. She put Benjy down and followed Mrs Willis into the kitchen.

'Now, tell me about the box. You've got me all curious.'

Molly suddenly felt a bit shy. She started to pull at the corner of her cardigan as she felt her cheeks go pink. Mrs Willis turned her back on Molly and wiped around the spotless sink. She started to hum.

'Actually, I want to make a special home for my toys.' Molly perched on a kitchen chair. 'So that I can hide them quickly . . .'

'Hide them! Why on earth would you want to do that?'

'In case the burglar comes back for them.' Molly sneaked a look at Mrs Willis.

'Molly, love, you mustn't fret about that horrible burglar. He won't ever come back again. The police will see to that.'

Molly put her elbows on the table and rested her chin in her hands. 'That's what Mum says, but why has she put more locks on the front door and special

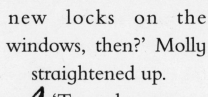

new locks on the windows, then?' Molly straightened up.

'To make sure no other person tries to get into your flat uninvited. Not even a thieving magpie,' she teased. 'The only way anyone is going to get into that flat is with your mum's keys. Your toys mustn't worry . . .'

'Mrs Willis,' Molly giggled. 'They're only toys, silly-billy.' Her laughter set Benjy off. He jumped into her lap and licked her ears. 'Ooh, that tickles, Benjy.'

Just then the doorbell rang. 'That'll be your mum wondering where you are,' said Mrs Willis. She went to open the door.

Molly groaned. 'I bet Aunt Jan's here,' she told Benjy. 'She's taking me to tea.'

18

She pulled a face. 'You understand how much I hate going out with boring Aunt Jan, don't you?'

Molly put Benjy in his basket and, with a dramatic sigh, went to the front door.

'Oh, Molly! You're covered in dog hair. Quick – go and change your clothes.'

'Don't make a fuss, Annie.' Aunt Jan gave a weak laugh and patted Molly on the head. 'She's fine as she is. Let's go, Molly.' Aunt Jan marched off to her car. Big, long strides that forget about children.

Molly put on her most sad and hurt face. She looked at her mother.

'Mu-um . . .'

'Mol-lee. Don't give me that. Jan loves you. You're the only thing she's got left to remind her of your dad. She's just not used to people your age. Please make an effort.'

Molly tutted loudly and stomped after Aunt Jan. Just as she reached the car, Molly suddenly remembered the box, which she'd left with Mrs Willis. 'Oops. Hang on, Aunt Jan.' She ran back to Mrs Willis's flat and rang the doorbell.

'Molly . . .'

'Actually, I don't think I need that box, Mrs Willis. You can have it. I don't want to hide my toys.' She stood on her tiptoes to give Mrs Willis a kiss, then ran back to the car.

Molly watched Aunt Jan put a dollop of thick cream on top of real-strawberry, strawberry jam, which dripped off a warm scone. She swallowed hard. Molly hated cream.

'There you go.' Aunt Jan shoved the scone under Molly's nose. 'Quick, Molly, before any more jam drips off.'

Molly licked her lips. Why hadn't she asked for chocolate cake? Molly tapped the table leg with her foot. She wished

Aunt Jan smiled more. She wished she didn't ask so many questions . . . She wished she wasn't scared of her.

'How's school, Molly?'

'All right.' Molly nibbled at her scone, trying to avoid the cream.

'And your best friend . . .'

Molly put the scone on her plate. 'Hannah. Her name is spelt the same . . .'

' . . . backwards!'

Molly looked at her unwanted scone. Aunt Jan never let her finish her sentences. 'Hannah's fine,' she mumbled sulkily.

Aunt Jan cleared her throat. 'Your neighbour seems to have quite a noisy little dog . . .'

'He's not noisy,' Molly cut in. 'Benjy's lovely, actually.' She stuck out her bottom lip and kicked the table leg harder. 'Mrs Willis is lovely, too.'

'Yes, I'm sure she is . . . Gosh, it's quite warm in here, isn't it? I wore my cardigan because the weather forecast said it might be a bit cooler today,' said Aunt Jan as she removed her cardigan. 'That's better.'

Molly looked up. She stared at Aunt Jan wide-eyed. She had been in such a sulky strop before that she hadn't noticed what Aunt Jan was wearing. Now she was entranced. She saw dazzling oranges and sunny yellows, like clean, thick paint

on new white paper. She longed to touch the warm, soft material, to rub it against her cheek. She would give anything to have such a lovely dress.

Molly wiped her sticky hands on her paper napkin. She looked at Aunt Jan's face. Really looked. For the first time she noticed Aunt Jan's thick brown hair and bright blue eyes. Just like her dad's. He had died before Molly was born, but she had a picture of him by her bedside lamp. Why had she never seen the likeness before.

'Molly? Are you all right?'

Molly blinked.

She cleared her throat.

'Aunt Jan, your dress is very beautiful.'

Aunt Jan looked straight at Molly, her mouth open. Then she smiled. She reached over to give Molly's hand a squeeze. 'That's the nicest thing anybody has ever said to me. Even nicer, as I made this dress.'

'You made it?' Now Molly's mouth was wide open.

Aunt Jan laughed. 'Careful – you'll catch flies!'

Molly couldn't believe anyone could make such a dress. 'It's much prettier than any dress from a shop – and it's in my favourite colours.'

Aunt Jan flushed pink from her neck to her ears.

'Now your face is as bright as your dress!' Molly quickly covered her mouth. She had never teased Aunt Jan before.

'Ooh, you cheeky monkey!' Aunt Jan laughed. It was a warm and friendly laugh. 'If you're not careful, I'll make you eat that cream, which you've so carefully avoided.' She dipped her finger in the cream bowl and put a splodge on Molly's nose.

Molly giggled, then looked at her cream scone. 'Aunt Jan, may I have some chocolate cake?'

Molly's stomach ached with laughter in the car on the way home. Aunt Jan was singing nursery rhymes and songs in silly voices.

Uh-oh. Molly suddenly realised she needed to go to the loo. The more she laughed, the more desperate she became.

She interrupted Donald Duck squawking Ten Green Bottles.

'Aunt Jan, are we nearly home?'

Aunt Jan stopped mid-verse. 'Oh, umm, yes.' Molly saw that she looked a bit hurt.

'Don't stop singing, Aunt Jan.' Molly forced a smile then continued to sing, 'Eight green bottles . . .'

As Aunt Jan took up the tune, Molly crossed her legs and concentrated hard. No, no, no, she cried inside. Just a bit longer . . . Molly hadn't wet herself for *ages*. Not in Aunt Jan's car, she begged.

It was no good. A warm, wet patch soaked through her skirt just as they pulled up outside the flat.

'Here we are,' Aunt Jan smiled, ruffling Molly's hair.

Molly blinked back hot tears. She looked up at her flat and saw her mother waving from the window.

'I'll just come up for a quick chat with your mum,' said Aunt Jan.

'OK,' said Molly in a quiet voice. She felt small inside. Now I've spoilt everything, she told herself. Please don't let Aunt Jan notice till I'm inside.

Molly waited until her mum had opened the front door. Then she ran straight to her room.

She was too ashamed to say goodbye to Aunt Jan.

'Molly, are you all right?' Her mum was standing outside the bedroom door. 'Jan said she had such fun with you. I think she was a bit hurt that you didn't say goodbye properly.'

'Mu-um,' Molly wailed, tears running down the corners of her wobbly mouth.

Molly's mum opened the door. 'Oh, Molly.' She cuddled up to her on the bed, careful not to squash James. 'If you really dislike going out with Aunt Jan so much, I won't make you see her again on your own.'

'But I like . . . Aunt . . . Jan,' Molly sniffed. 'She's got a beautiful dress . . . and soft hair . . . and lovely eyes. But she hates me now.' Molly let out a big, huffy sob.

'Of course she doesn't hate . . .'

'I wet myself in her car,' Molly wailed.

Her mum stroked her hair. 'You silly-billy. Is that all?'

Two days later a letter arrived for Molly.

Dear Molly

I had a lovely day on Sunday. I've still got a stitch in my side from laughing so much. Sorry I didn't get a chance to thank you — you ran off so quickly.

See you next Sunday?

No cream, I promise.

Love

Aunt Jan

PS I nearly wet myself laughing, too.

Next time, SHOUT!

3 Four go fishing!

'Molly, you bring the bucket with the two fishing-lines in it,' Tim shouted. The water lapped round his shins as he held on to the side of the boat, whilst Rosie fiddled with the engine.

Molly skipped down the sandy beach to the water's edge, which wasn't very easy in her wellington boots. She clutched the large, smelly bucket in both hands. She knew that if she dropped it the fishing-lines could get into a terribly knotty mess.

'OK, I'll take the bucket,' said Tim, 'and your mum can pass you over to me.'

'Actually, I can get in by myself,' said Molly, sloshing into the sea and accidentally splashing Tim. He raised an eyebrow. 'It's only water, silly-billy.' Molly clambered into the boat, grabbing Rosie's outstretched hand to haul herself in.

The little rowing boat just fitted the three adults and Molly. 'Tim,' Molly giggled, 'I hope there'll be room in your boat for all the fish we catch.'

'So do I, Molly,' Tim agreed. 'Or someone will be swimming home.'

'And it won't be me,' Molly's mum chipped in. 'It may be a warm, sunny summer's day, but this water is freezing.'

'I doubt any of us will need to swim back,' Rosie laughed. 'Tim and I have

been out every
day for five days
before you two arrived and we've
only caught three mackerel and a crab.'

'That's because we didn't have the expert here, with her brand new fishing-rod,' said Tim. 'Isn't that right, Molly?'

Molly loved fishing. She never used to like fish; it didn't seem sensible to eat food which smelled like James's supper. But fish straight from the sea, which Molly caught herself, wasn't like oily chunks from a tin or sloppy-sicky fish pie. It was a prize – better than the coconut shy at the fair – and it was delicious. The freezer at home was just about empty of all the mackerel they'd caught the last time she and her mum had come up to Scotland with Tim and Rosie.

'OK everyone. Hold tight whilst I start up the engine,' said Rosie. 'Cross your fingers, Molly. It's a bit temperamental this year.'

Molly tried to work out how to hold tight whilst crossing her fingers, and Rosie pulled the cord to start the engine.

'Wha-hey!' cried Tim as the engine caught first time.

'That must be a good sign,' called Molly's mum.

The little boat sped off over the blue-green waves.

Half an hour later, Molly had already caught two mackerel. 'One for me and one for James,' she said.

Tim gutted the fish and threw the heads and innards to the gulls circling above.

'You're right about the expert,' Rosie teased Tim.

'Hmm,' said Tim. He sounded a little grouchy.

Rosie winked at Molly.

When Molly had caught four more and her mum two, her mum suggested they give Tim and Rosie a turn.

'Tim can use my lucky line,' Molly offered.

It was clearly only lucky for Molly, though. All Tim caught was a nasty jellyfish tentacle.

'Shouldn't you wear gloves?' asked Molly, watching Tim as he tried to remove the tentacle from the hook.

'Ouch!' he yelled. Molly's mum and Rosie sniggered. 'Yes, you're quite right, Molly,' he said, forcing a smile.

'I tell you what,' said Molly's mum. 'Let's try beyond that point. There's bound to be something there – that's where we caught so many last year.'

'Good idea. Ooh, hang on – I think I've got a nibble. Feels like quite a big fellow,' Rosie puffed as she reeled the line in.

'Hey, you've got two, Rosie,' Molly cried, delighted.

Rosie gave Tim a smug smile. She turned to Molly. 'Why don't you sit next to me and steer the boat?'

'And I'll trawl a line as we go,' said Tim, who was determined not to be the only one without a catch.

'Yes,' said Rosie. 'Otherwise you'll be without supper tonight.' Tim threw a fish head at her.

Molly loved to steer. Except she always got confused, because to go right she had to push the rudder left, and to go left she had to push it right.

'You'll have to shout left and right, though,' Molly warned them.

'LEFT AND RIGHT!' they all shouted.

Molly groaned. 'Silly-billies. Not yet!'

As they neared the point, Tim suddenly yelled, 'Hey, look!'

'You've caught something!' said Molly hopefully. She didn't want Tim to feel left out.

'No. Look over there.' Tim pointed towards the big buoy off the point.

'It's just the buoy . . .' said Rosie.

'No – there.'

'What is it?' asked Molly's mum, who could also see something in the water ahead.

'I don't know. I can only make out the fin,' said Tim, quickly hauling in his line. 'Let's get closer.'

Molly's heart started to pound. She wasn't so keen on big fish. Fins meant sharks. Sharks meant . . .

'Molly, steer left.' Tim was tense with excitement. 'Where's the camera?' Molly's mum passed it to him.

'Mum?' Molly looked pleadingly at her.

'There's nothing to be afraid of, Molly.'

'Perhaps I should steer this bit. What do you think?' Rosie asked.

Molly nodded. She sat on her hands to stop them shaking. Any minute now a huge, great, toothy shark is going to leap out of the water. Why do we have to get closer? Perhaps I can throw the shark the fish I've caught . . . James will understand . . .

Molly swallowed hard and watched as the fin came closer, getting bigger and bigger . . . Noooo! She couldn't watch. She scrunched up her shoulders and squeezed her eyes shut ready for . . .

'AAARGH!' Rosie's hand was on her shoulder.

'It's OK,' Rosie laughed. 'It won't eat you.'

Rosie cut the engine, so as not to scare the fin away. Molly could only hear the waves lapping against the boat. She looked back at the shore. It was far away. The sea was so big; their boat so small . . . Who would come to their rescue?

'Oh, look!' Molly's mum pointed to the fin, which was now about two metres from the boat.

Molly gasped, eyes now wide open with fear . . . Then she smiled: 'A dolphin!'

'Not a dolphin,' said Tim, snapping away with his camera. 'It's a porpoise.'

'It's just a baby,' Molly breathed as the porpoise splashed out of the water then dived under again. She leant over the side of the boat and trailed her hand in the water. If only it would come closer, she could stroke its smooth grey skin. How could I have been so scared of you?

'Bet you thought it was some killer shark,' said her mum, winking.

'I was a bit scared,' she admitted shyly.

Tim ruffled her hair. 'It's more likely to be scared of us. Four noisy people in a rickety old boat. It's no wonder you don't see many porpoises here any more, with so many fishing boats and ferries and submarines about.'

'You really are a lucky person to have on board, Molly,' Rosie smiled.

'I wonder why it's all on its own,' said Tim.

'I hope it's not lost,' said Molly sadly. It would be scary to be alone in the sea, she thought.

The porpoise surfaced once more near the boat as if to say goodbye, then disappeared out of sight.

'Yes, go and find your friends,' said Molly, waving. 'Don't get left behind.'

They watched the grey-blue waves in silence for a few moments. Molly imagined the porpoises and mackerel and jellyfish swimming under the boat. She smiled to herself. My porpoise isn't alone.

'Well, I think we've done enough fishing,' said Tim.

'*We?*' cried Molly's mum and Rosie.

'You mean Molly, Annie and me,' corrected Rosie as she started up the engine.

Tim looked sheepish. 'Well . . .'

'But Tim saw the porpoise,' said Molly, 'and he *caught* it on camera!'

Her mum and Rosie groaned, but Tim looked smug. 'And that comes from the expert!' he beamed.

4 *A surprise for Molly*

'Hannah's got a new dress.'

'Has she indeed.'

'Mum ...?'

'Molly ...?'

'It's Emma's birthday on Saturday and ...'

'I know, Molly.' Molly's mum stopped tapping away at her computer and turned round to face her. 'OK. I suppose you could do with a smart new dress.

We've run out of hand-me-downs to fit you - you're growing so fast. I'll take you to Harvey's tomorrow after school.'

Molly kissed her mum on the nose. 'Thank you, Mum.' She skipped along to her bedroom. She picked up James, who had been sleeping peacefully on her bed, and danced him round and round the room. 'A brand new dress, James!'

Molly had never chosen a dress of her own before. She had two older cousins, Tess, who was eleven, and Lizzie, who was nine, and she had always been dressed in their cast offs. Molly didn't mind – she wasn't that interested in clothes – but now that she had seen Hannah's new dress, she was desperate for one of her own.

As she waited for Saturday to come, Molly daydreamed about what to choose.

Nothing too long or too straight. She must be able to run about in it and play musical chairs.

Nothing too plain and dull – dark blue or dark green, like a boring old school uniform.

Nothing like Hannah's. Molly liked the pretty pale blue and yellow flowers, but they weren't nearly bright enough.

Molly wanted a dress as warm as the dancing flames of a bonfire; a dress that dazzled like the hot summer sun reflected on a clear, blue sea. A dress as beautiful as Aunt Jan's.

Molly loved Harvey's department store. All the shiny-clean pots and pans in the basement, fabrics and ribbons and buttons on the second floor, even the neat, well-behaved uniforms on the fourth floor. Best of all, though, she loved the fifth floor. She could happily spend hours browsing along aisle after aisle of toys and games and books. It even had its own reading-corner with colourful beanbags and tables which were at just the right height.

Usually it was a treat to visit Harvey's. Today, though, her mum was in a bad mood. Molly had a sinking feeling in her stomach as she looked at the tight, no-nonsense expression on her mum's face. She tugged at her mum's hand as they went through the revolving doors.

'Mum . . . ?'

'No, we're not going to the fifth floor.

We're going straight to the clothes section, straight to the rail of dresses and straight out again, OK?'

'Actually, I wasn't even going to mention the fifth floor,' Molly sulked, cross that Mum had guessed right.

'Oh really? What were you going to say?'

'It doesn't matter any more.'

Molly's mum stopped, bent down and stared at Molly's face. 'Do I see a sticking-out lip? Are you sulking, madam?'

'No,' said Molly in a small voice.

'Because if you are,' said her mum straightening up, 'we're going home right this minute. Understand?'

Molly nodded, but her mum didn't notice because she was already dragging Molly towards the escalator.

Better keep quiet, Molly told herself as they went up the escalator. Molly knew her mum didn't like to talk when she was in a scratchy mood.

Molly hopped off the top step before it gobbled her toes. She pulled at her mum's hand again — she'd been quiet long enough.

'Mum?'

'Hmm?'

'I want a dress as beautiful as Aunt Jan's.'

'You want, eh? What about "would like" and "please"? Money doesn't grow on trees.'

Molly looked at her toes. She hated it when Mum talked about money.

'I know, Mum. I didn't mean . . .'

'Come on. Here's the children's section. Let's make it quick. I'm not in the mood for silliness.' She let go of Molly's hand.

Molly looked up at the rails of clothes. There were dresses of every kind. Long ones, straight ones, plain ones and fancy ones. Dresses with polka dots and stripes, animals and flowers. Dresses with ribbons and bows and matching hats.

She swallowed hard. Suddenly she knew she wouldn't find a

dress like Aunt Jan's. Not today. Not when her mum was in such a bad mood.

Molly's mum was already at a rail of dresses. She had picked out a plain, navy blue dress at least two sizes too big for Molly. 'What about this one? It'll hide any mess you make, and it will last.'

Molly looked at her mum's expression to see if she was joking. She wasn't. Molly stuck her bottom lip out.

'Miss Sulk, are we going to be difficult?'

'No!' Molly turned away, furious. She hated to be called that. 'I'm not sulking.'

'O-K . . . What about this one?'

Molly burst into tears. Choosing a beautiful dress should be special. Molly couldn't do it when her mum was in a horrible, hurry-hurry, no fun mood. Nothing looked pretty now. Her mum had ruined everything.

'It's ug-lee,' she wailed. Tears poured down her cheeks. She snatched the dress and threw it on the floor. 'I hate it! And I hate you!'

Nearby, a sales assistant cleared her throat. Molly was suddenly aware of the people around her. The little boy staring at her, finger in mouth . . . The young woman pretending not to notice . . . The elderly couple tut-tutting. It made Molly even more cross — her mum was showing her up in front of all these people and in her favourite shop.

Molly's mum picked the dress up and shoved it back on the rail. She grabbed Molly's arm, fingers digging deep and marched Molly down the escalator and out of the shop.

Molly tried to wipe the tears from her eyes, but it was very difficult to do that and concentrate on not tripping over – her mum was walking so fast.

She felt very small.

Back home, Molly curled up next to James on the bed and told him what had happened.

'Mum's a real meanie, James. If I can't have a dress like Aunt Jan's, I don't want one at all. It doesn't have to cost lots of money, it just has to be . . . special. You understand, don't you?' James blinked at Molly. He seemed to understand. 'It's not fair. Whenever Mum buys new clothes she takes ages. And we have to go to every shop so that she can try on every dress or skirt or pair of trousers before she makes up her mind.' She scratched behind James's ears. 'I'm never speaking to Mum again and I'm never going shopping with her again.' James looked at her. 'I mean it. I'm only going to talk to you.'

An hour before Molly had to leave for Emma's birthday party, she put on a clean yellow T-shirt and stripy blue-and-white leggings. 'Not very special,' she told James, who was asleep on the windowsill because the bed was covered in discarded clothes, 'but at least I'm colourful. Anyway, I'm not wearing Tess's boring old dress which pinches under the arms.'

There was a knock on her bedroom door. Molly looked at the door and stuck out her tongue.

'Mol-lee . . . are you going to let me in?'

Molly plonked herself on her bed and crossed her arms. It had been three days since the shopping trip. She still hadn't spoken to her mum.

'This is getting silly, Molly.' Her mum sighed. 'If you carry on behaving like a baby, I shan't give you this surprise . . .'

Surprise! Molly uncrossed her arms and crept to the door.

'What is it?' she tried to sound

uninterested as she squinted through the key hole.

'Are we talking?' Molly glanced at James. He was still asleep. She shrugged. After three days, she missed having a proper conversation. Molly opened the door.

'It's a present from Aunt Jan,' said her mum, handing her a parcel. Molly couldn't be cross any more. A present – and it wasn't even her birthday. She unwrapped the parcel, careful not to tear the paper, which was yellow – her favourite colour – with pretty white daisies all over it. She gasped. 'It's exactly like Aunt Jan's dress.'

She held the dress against her body, stroking the fabric. She smiled up at her mum, eyes sparkling. Then she tore off her T-shirt and leggings, put on the dress and gave a twirl.

Her mum moved some clothes off the bed and sat down. She reached out for Molly and held her hands. 'Aunt Jan told me what a lovely thing you said to her about her dress . . .' Molly could feel herself going hot in the face. '. . . and I realised why you were so keen to have a special dress.' She pulled Molly closer and gave her a hug. 'Shopping for your dress should have been a treat, and I spoilt it with my bad mood. Am I forgiven?'

'Of course you are,' Molly grinned. 'But, Mum, you're squashing my beautiful new dress – and we're going to be late for the party!'

'That's the rest of the surprise. Why don't you look outside . . .'

Molly didn't wait for her mum to finish. She ran to the hall and opened the front door.

'Aunt Jan!' she squealed, then suddenly felt shy. She walked up to Aunt Jan who was sitting in her car, wearing the same dress as Molly. 'Thank you for my dress. It's just like yours.'

'Does that make us twins?' Aunt Jan asked.

Molly smiled and nodded. She got into the car and put on the seatbelt.

'Aunt Jan, will you take me to Emma's party, please?'